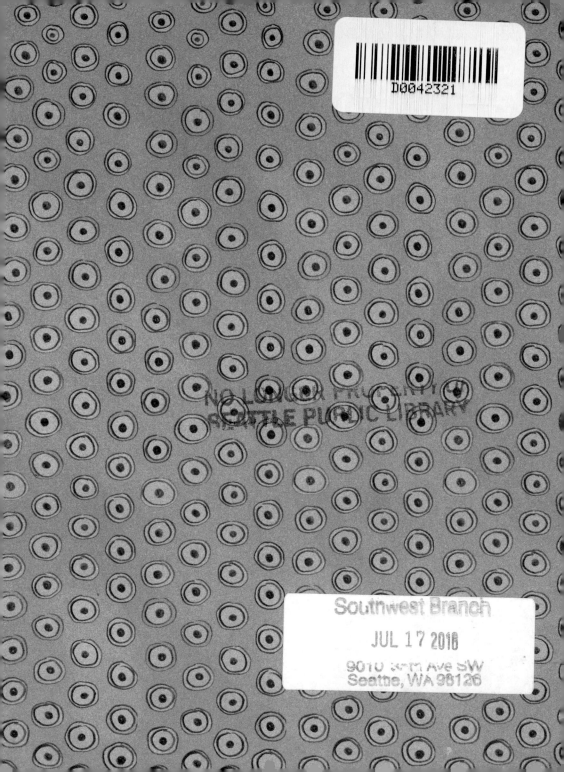

D0042321

NO LONGER PROPERTY OF
SEATTLE PUBLIC LIBRARY

Southwest Branch

JUL 17 2018

9010 35th Ave SW
Seattle, WA 98126

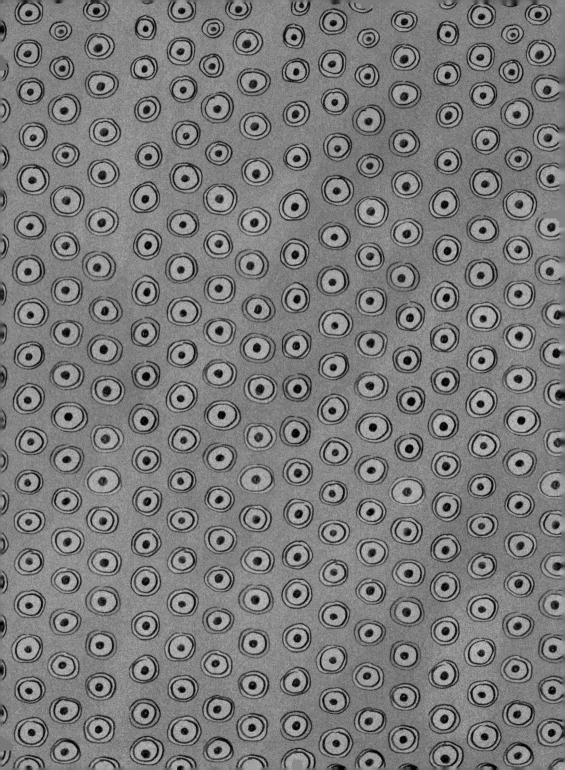

THE TRUTH ABOUT MY UNBELIEVABLE SUMMER...

For Sibilla and Morgana
—Davide

For Jules
—Benjamin

Text copyright © 2016 by Davide Cali.
Illustrations copyright © 2016 by Benjamin Chaud.

All rights reserved. No part of this book may be reproduced
in any form without written permission from the publisher.

Library of Congress Cataloging-in-Publication Data available.

ISBN 978-1-4521-4483-2

Manufactured in China.

Design by Ryan Hayes.
Typeset in 1820 Modern.

10 9 8 7 6 5 4 3 2 1

Chronicle Books LLC
680 Second Street
San Francisco, California 94107

Chronicle Books—we see things differently.
Become part of our community at www.chroniclekids.com.

THE TRUTH ABOUT MY UNBELIEVABLE SUMMER...

Davide Cali   Benjamin Chaud

chronicle books · san francisco

Well, you may not believe this, but ...

I found a message in a bottle. It wasn't just any message—it was a treasure map!

Then a magpie pecked it out of my hands!

So I chased the bird all the way onto a ship in port.

Apparently, the crew didn't appreciate unexpected guests.

Just when I thought I'd escaped,
I almost became a giant squid's lunch.

Luckily, I was rescued by a submarine captain . . .

Who promptly put me to work.

When the submarine finally surfaced,
we had traveled back in time!

"How did *that* happen?"

It didn't. Actually, it was just some
people making a movie.

Then, by chance, I met an actress who
knew exactly where to find my map!

It was just a little out of reach . . .

Anyway, the treasure hunt was back on!

But something went wrong . . .

And I ended up in the desert.

It turns out that my arrival disturbed some deep sleepers.

At just the right moment,
my uncle passed by in his latest invention.

Since it was still experimental, there were some surprises.

My uncle dropped me off on a deserted island, where the magpie stole my map *again*.

"Was it really
the same bird?"

Yes! I have no idea how it found me!

I chased that bird everywhere.

And I mean, *everywhere.*

At last, I had it!

So I hitched a ride down the mountain.

And then I remembered my uncle's jet pack!

Once airborne, it was easy to follow the map's directions.
X marked the spot . . .

Back where I started! And I couldn't believe it . . .

This was the treasure?!

Still, I guess my summer was OK.

So you probably don't believe me . . . right?

Three months earlier . . .

- The End -

Davide Cali is an author, illustrator, and cartoonist who has published more than 40 books, including *I Didn't Do My Homework Because . . .*, *A Funny Thing Happened on the Way to School . . .*, and *I Didn't Do My Homework Because Doodle Book of Excuses*. He lives in France and Italy.

Benjamin Chaud has illustrated more than 60 books. He is the illustrator of *I Didn't Do My Homework Because . . .*, *A Funny Thing Happened on the Way to School . . .*, and *I Didn't Do My Homework Because Doodle Book of Excuses*. He is the author and illustrator of New York Times Notable Book *The Bear's Song*, *The Bear's Sea Escape*, *The Bear's Surprise*, and *Farewell Floppy*, as well as the Pomelo series. He lives in Die, France.

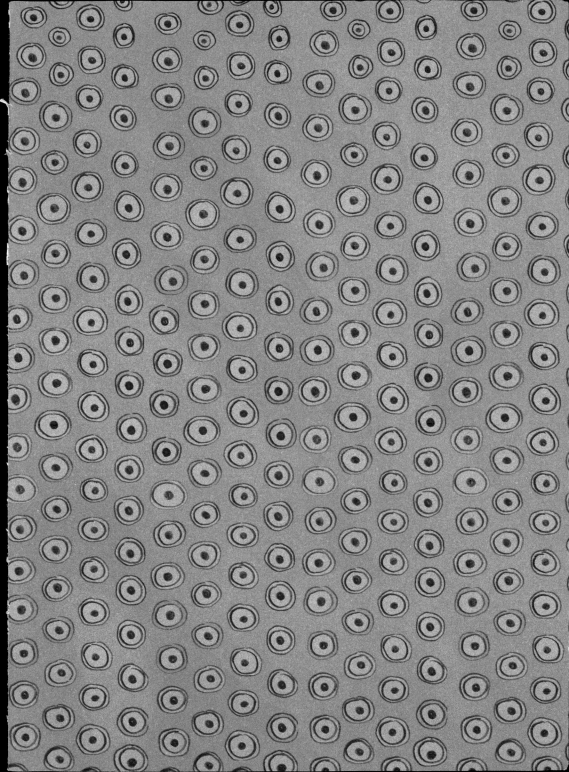

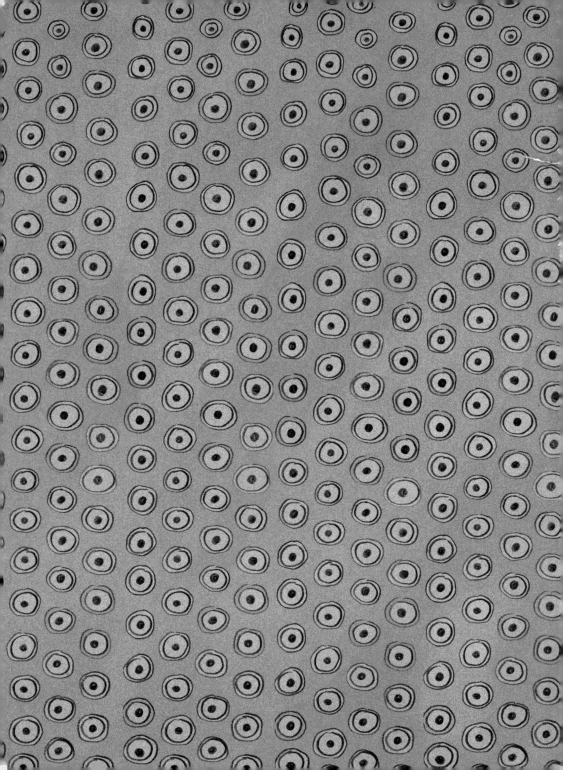